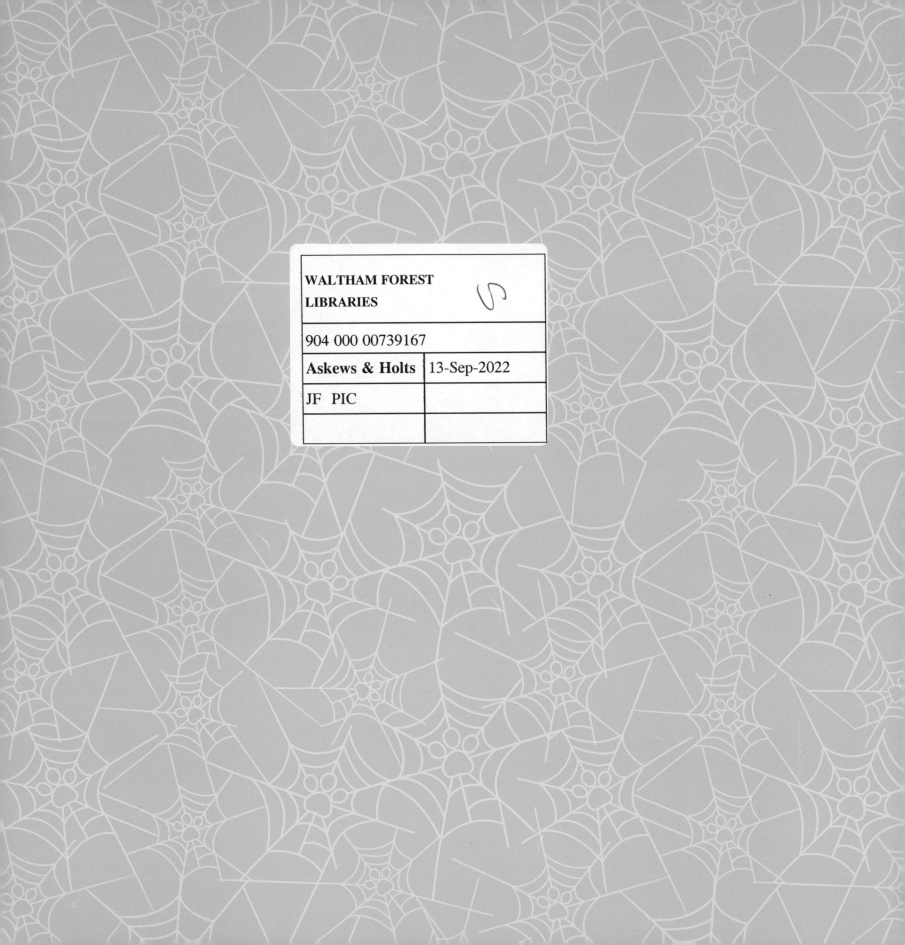

This storybook belongs to

....

First published in Great Britain 2022 by Farshore
An imprint of HarperCollins*Publishers*
1 London Bridge Street, London SE1 9GF
www.farshore.co.uk

HarperCollins*Publishers*
1st Floor, Watermarque Building, Ringsend Road
Dublin 4, Ireland

ISBN 978 0 0085 3222 2
Printed in Great Britain by Bell and Bain Ltd, Glasgow
001

A CIP catalogue record for this title is available from the British Library.

MIX
Paper from
responsible sources
FSC® C007454

FSC
www.fsc.org

HALLOWEEN HEROES!

It was Halloween at the Lookout, and the PAW Patrol was excitedly preparing for the big night.

"Dressing up in costume is my favourite part of Halloween," said Princess Skye.

"My favourite part is trick-or-treating!" said Pirate Zuma. "Arr!"

But there was one thing they agreed on: they were both looking forward to Cap'n Turbot's ghost ship party!

"It sounds super scary."

"Aww, that's only scary if you believe in ghosts," Zuma replied. Suddenly, they heard a spooky wailing sound, and a ghost fluttered down next to Zuma! The pirate pup yelped and jumped into the air.

"That's not a real ghost," Skye said
with a giggle. "That's just Chase
hanging a decoration."
"Told you there's no such thing as ghosts,"
Zuma said, though he was shaking.

Outside the Lookout, Rocky, Marshall and Rubble had found a huge pumpkin to carve. Rocky cut the top with his Super Jack-o'-Lantern Scooper, and Marshall tried to pull it off. He tugged and tugged until it popped off the pumpkin ...

... and landed on Rubble's head!

"This goo in my hairdo makes me blue," said Rubble with a chuckle.

Meanwhile, Cap'n Turbot welcomed his first guests to the old pirate ship. Mayor Goodway and Chickaletta, Katie and Cali, and Mr Porter and his grandson, Alex, all wore wonderful costumes.

Mr Porter had brought delicious Halloween cookies, and everyone told Cap'n Turbot they liked the spooky way he had decorated the boat.

"Thank you," he said. "Just trying to be the host with the most ghosts. Legend has it that this pirate vessel once sailed the waters of Adventure Bay with a ghost crew! Mwah-ha-ha-ha!"

Alex was a little scared. He tugged at his grandpa's sleeve. "Is the ship really haunted?" he asked.

"No," said Mr Porter. "It's fun to play at being scared sometimes. There's no such thing as ghosts."

But if there were no ghosts on board, Mr Porter wondered, who had eaten all his Halloween cookies?

And Katie wondered what was making that spooky moaning sound.

Later, while Cali was chasing a pesky seagull around the ship, she accidentally pulled on a rope that raised a sail.

Mayor Goodway was spooked. "Why is that sail going up on its own?" she asked.

Then the ship started to move! As the boat sailed away, the gangplank collapsed and Cap'n Turbot fell into the water! The pirate ship was headed out to sea – with no one at the helm!

"I seem to have misplaced my glasses in the ocean," Cap'n Turbot said, rushing to climb back on board. But without his glasses, he couldn't steer the boat.

This was a job for the PAW Patrol! Mr Porter called for help, and Ryder assembled the team.
"Strange things are happening at Cap'n Turbot's Halloween party," he said. "Zuma, I need you and your hovercraft to catch up with the runaway ship."
"Let's dive in!" barked the pirate pup.

"Skye, I need you and your helicopter to help
slow down the ship," Ryder added. "And, Marshall,
I need you to ride in Skye's harness to help lower the sails."
The team was ready for a ruff-ruff rescue!

Ryder and Zuma raced across the water as Skye zoomed through the air, carrying Marshall. When they reached the pirate ship, Skye slowed down and Marshall swung into the crow's nest!
Everyone cheered when Marshall lowered the sails.

At the same time, Ryder and Zuma raced alongside the ship. Ryder climbed out of his ATV and onto a ladder. But when Zuma jumped, he missed and splashed into the sea!

Luckily, he had propellers on his Pup Pack. He turned them on and shot out of the water – right into Ryder's arms!

The pirate ship was rocking and turning through the waves as if someone was sailing it!

"A ghost must be doing it," said Alex.
"That is so cool!"

Alex might have thought being on a ghost ship was cool, but Ryder wasn't convinced.

"There's got to be a simple explanation for all this," he said. "Let's check out the steering wheel."

But Zuma and Marshall didn't budge.

"Oh," said Zuma, looking around for ghosts. "You meant us, too."

When Ryder, Zuma and Marshall went to investigate, they made a surprising discovery: Chickaletta was perched on the wheel, turning it back and forth! "There's your Halloween ghost," Ryder said, laughing. Zuma and Marshall sighed with relief.

But as Ryder was taking Chickaletta back to Mayor Goodway, a spooky moan came from behind some old barrels. Everyone was scared, but Ryder boldly walked towards the barrels.

Marshall and Zuma tried to stop him. "Ryder, don't!" they pleaded.

Ryder looked into the shadows and found ...

WOOOOH!

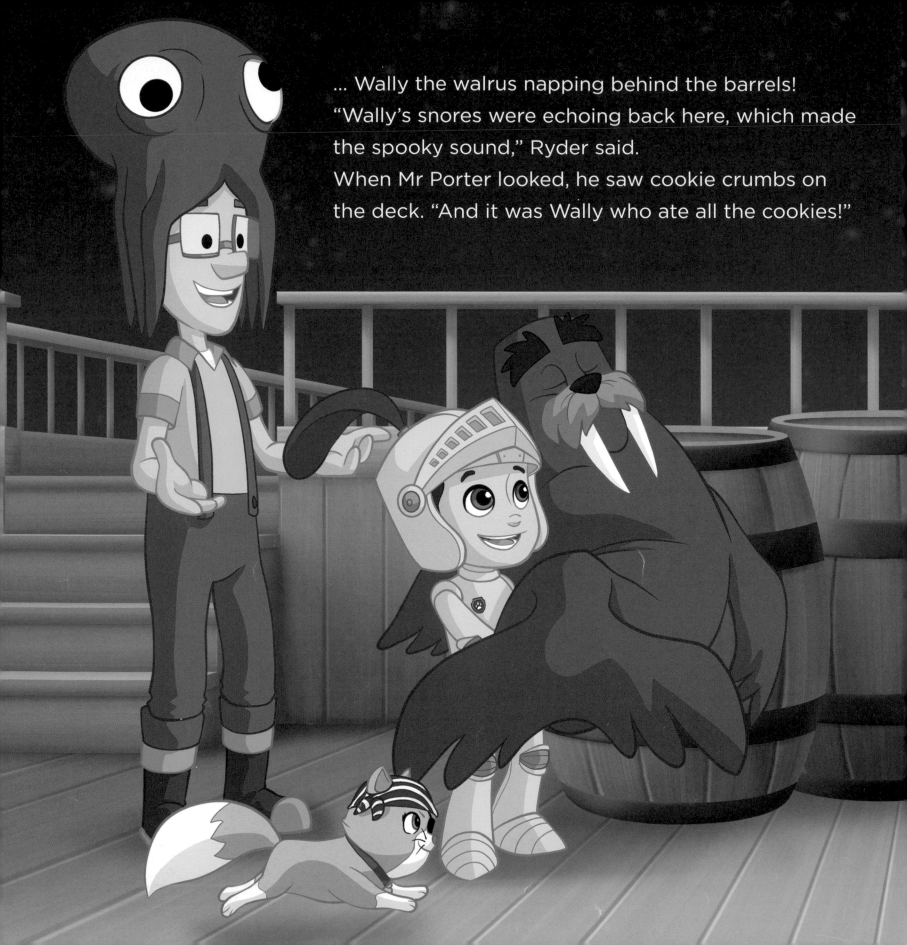

... Wally the walrus napping behind the barrels!
"Wally's snores were echoing back here, which made the spooky sound," Ryder said.
When Mr Porter looked, he saw cookie crumbs on the deck. "And it was Wally who ate all the cookies!"

Just then, Cali ran by, chasing the seagull. Once again, she accidentally raised the sail – but this time, the others saw it happen.

"Chickaletta was our secret captain. Wally the walrus made the ghostly sounds. And Cali raised the sails," Ryder said. He had solved all the mysteries! He even helped Cap'n Turbot find his glasses ... in his pocket!

Once they all got to dry land, they moved the party to the Lookout. There were games and treats for everyone. And best of all, the fun was ghost-free! Then Rocky looked up and saw something amazing.

A glowing pirate ship seemed to be floating across the full moon!
"I'm sure there's a simple explanation – I just don't know what it is!" said Ryder. "Happy Halloween, everyone!"

THE END

A REVVED-UP RACING ADVENTURE

Join the pit-crew **PAW Patrol** pups as they work together to keep race day on track. Meet you at the finish line! **READY, RACE, RESCUE!**

ISBN: 978-0-00-852626-9